Merry 1st Christmas our sweet Phoebe!

Love you

Grandma and Grandpa
Russell

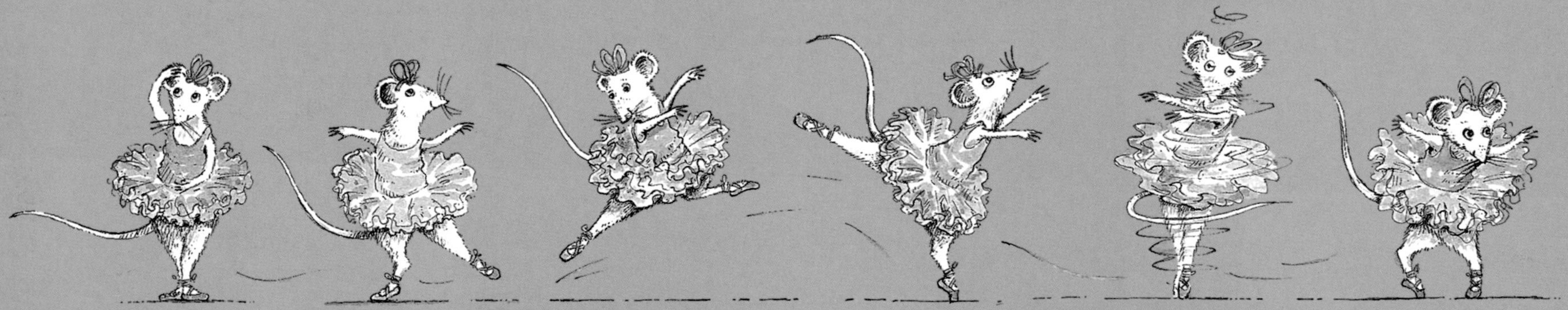

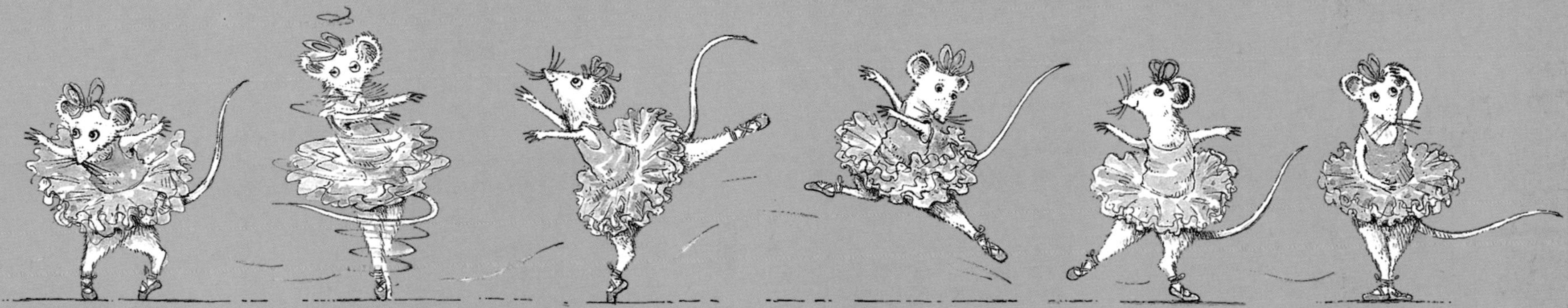

For Tara KH

To my aunt, Catherine Hope Beddington, with love HC

VIKING
Published by Penguin Group
Penguin Young Readers Group, 345 Hudson Street, New York, New York 10014, U.S.A.
Penguin Group (Canada), 90 Eglinton Avenue East, Suite 700, Toronto, Ontario, Canada M4P 2Y3 (a division of Pearson Penguin Canada Inc.)
Penguin Books Ltd, 80 Strand, London WC2R 0RL, England
Penguin Ireland, 25 St Stephen's Green, Dublin 2, Ireland (a division of Penguin Books Ltd)
Penguin Group (Australia), 250 Camberwell Road, Camberwell, Victoria 3124, Australia (a division of Pearson Australia Group Pty Ltd)
Penguin Books India Pvt Ltd, 11 Community Centre, Panchsheel Park, New Delhi – 110 017, India
Penguin Group (NZ), 67 Apollo Drive, Rosedale, North Shore 0632, New Zealand (a division of Pearson New Zealand Ltd.)
Penguin Books (South Africa) (Pty) Ltd, 24 Sturdee Avenue, Rosebank, Johannesburg 2196, South Africa

Penguin Books Ltd, Registered Offices: 80 Strand, London WC2R 0RL, England

First published in Great Britain by Aurum Press, 1983
First published in the United States of America by Clarkson N. Potter, 1983
This edition published by Viking, a division of Penguin Young Readers Group, 2008

7 9 10 8 6

THE LIBRARY OF CONGRESS HAS CATALOGED THE PLEASANT COMPANY EDITION AS FOLLOWS:
Craig, Helen.
Angelina ballerina / illustrations by Helen Craig ;
story by Katharine Holabird
p. cm.
Summary: Angelina loves to dance and wants to become a ballerina more than anything else in the world.
ISBN: 1-58485-655-6
[1. Mice—Fiction. 2. Ballet dancing—Fiction. 3. Dancers—Fiction.]
I. Holabird, Katharine. II. Title. PZ7.C84418 An 2000
[E]—dc21 00-022882

This edition ISBN 978-0-670-01117-9

Manufactured in China
Set in Bembo

Angelina Ballerina

Story by **Katharine Holabird** Illustrations by **Helen Craig**

VIKING

More than anything else in the world, Angelina loved to dance. She danced all the time and she danced everywhere, and often she was so busy dancing that she forgot about the other things she was supposed to be doing.

Angelina's mother was always calling to her, "Angelina, it's time to tidy up your room now," or "Please get ready for school now, Angelina." But Angelina never wanted to go to school. She never wanted to do anything but dance.

One night Angelina even danced in her dreams, and
when she woke up in the morning, she knew that
she was going to be a real ballerina someday.

When Mrs. Mouseling called Angelina for breakfast,
Angelina was standing on her bed doing curtsies.

When it was time for school, Angelina was trying on her mother's hats and making sad and funny faces at herself in the mirror. "You're going to be late again, Angelina!" cried Mrs. Mouseling.

But Angelina did
not care. She skipped
over rocks

and practiced high
leaps over the
flower beds until
she landed right in

old Mrs. Hodgepodge's
pansies and got a
terrible scolding.

At playtime she twirled and spun across the playground so fast that none of the little boys in her class could catch her, and they were all very annoyed.

After school she did a beautiful arabesque in the kitchen and knocked over a pitcher of milk and a plate of her mother's best cheddar-cheese pies.

"Oh Angelina, your dancing is nothing but a nuisance!"
exclaimed her mother.

She sent Angelina straight upstairs to her room and went
to have a talk with Mr. Mouseling. Mrs. Mouseling
shook her head and said, "I just don't know what to do
about Angelina." Mr. Mouseling thought awhile and
then he said, "I think I may have an idea."

That same afternoon, Mr. and Mrs. Mouseling
went out together before the shops closed.

The next morning at breakfast, Angelina
found a large box with her name on it.

Inside the box was a pink ballet dress and a pair of pink
ballet slippers. Angelina's father smiled at her kindly.
"I think you are ready to take ballet lessons," he said.

Angelina was so excited that she jumped straight up in the
air and landed with one foot in her mother's sewing basket.

The very next day Angelina took her pink slippers and ballet dress and went to her first lesson at Miss Lilly's Ballet School. There were nine other little girls in the class and they all practiced curtsies and pliés and ran around the room together just like fairies. Then they skipped and twirled about until it was time to go home.

"Congratulations, Angelina," said Miss Lilly. "You are a good little dancer and if you work hard, you may grow up to be a real ballerina one day."

Angelina ran all the way home to give her mother a big hug.
"I'm the happiest little girl in the world today!" she said.

From that day on, Angelina came downstairs when her mother called her, she tidied her room, and she went to school on time.

She helped her mother
make cheddar-cheese pies

and she even let the boys catch her
on the playground sometimes.

Angelina was so busy dancing at Miss Lilly's that she
didn't need to dance at suppertime or bedtime or on
the way to school anymore. She went every day to her
ballet lessons and worked very hard for many years…

...until at last she became the famous ballerina Mademoiselle Angelina, and people came from far and wide to enjoy her lovely dancing.